I SPY

AN EGG IN A NEST

For Owen, Kei, Grace, and Will,
with thanks to Dan and Dave
—J.M.

For Agnes Sallick
—W.W.

Text copyright © 2011 by Jean Marzollo.
Cover illustration (and first spread) "Nature" from *I Spy: a Book of Picture Riddles* © 1992 by Walter Wick; "Into the Woods" from *I Spy Fantasy* © 1994 by Walter Wick; "Prizes to Win" from *I Spy Fun House* © 1993 by Walter Wick; "Clouds" from *I Spy Fantasy* © 1994 by Walter Wick; "The Golden Cage" from *I Spy Mystery* © 1993 by Walter Wick; "The Rainbow Express" from *I Spy Fantasy* © 1994 by Walter Wick; "Puppet Theater" from *I Spy Fun House* © 1993 by Walter Wick; "Silhouettes" from *I Spy: A Book of Picture Riddles* © 1992 by Walter Wick; "View from the Fort" from *I Spy Treasure Hunt* © 1999 by Walter Wick; "Toys in the Attic" from *I Spy: A Book of Picture Riddles* © 1992 by Walter Wick.

All rights reserved. Published by Scholastic Inc.
SCHOLASTIC, CARTWHEEL BOOKS, and associated logos
are trademarks and/or registered trademarks of Scholastic Inc.
Lexile is a registered trademark of MetaMetrics, Inc.

Library of Congress Cataloging-in-Publication Data
Marzollo, Jean.
I spy an egg in a nest / by Jean Marzollo ; photographs by Walter Wick.
p. cm. -- (Scholastic reader. Level 1)
ISBN 978-0-545-22093-4
1. Picture puzzles--Juvenile literature. I. Wick, Walter, ill. II. Title. III. Series.
GV1507.P47M2924 2011
793.73--dc22
2009051611

ISBN 978-0-545-22093-4

10 9 8 7   14 15
Printed in the U.S.A. 40 • First printing, January 2011

SCHOLASTIC READER
LEVEL 1
50-250 WORDS

I SPY

AN EGG IN A NEST

Riddles by Jean Marzollo
Photographs by Walter Wick

Cartwheel
·B·O·O·K·S·®

SCHOLASTIC INC.
New York Toronto London Auckland
Sydney Mexico City New Delhi Hong Kong

I spy

a butterfly,

two small stones,

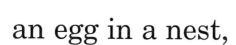

an egg in a nest,

and two pinecones.

I spy

a tire,

antlers,

a skunk,

and a woman who lives
inside a tree trunk.

I spy

 a flamingo,

a red bull's-eye,

 a yellow umbrella,

and a blue bow tie.

I spy

a flag,

an angel's wing,

 a unicorn's horn,

a hat,

and a string.

I spy

a cactus,

 a tiny door,

a painted flower,

and a real one on the floor.

I spy

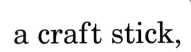

a craft stick,

a cave's yellow glow,

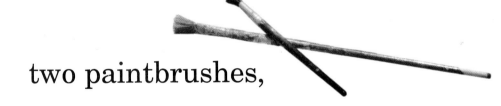

two paintbrushes,

and a pretty rainbow.

I spy

a cane,

 a lamb,

a red ball,

 a W block,

and a dog that's small.

I spy

 a fireman,

a gear,

 a dragon,

a baseball player's glove,

and a little toy wagon.

I spy

a picnic table,

 a little tan dog,

a man with blue yarn,

 and a peaceful frog.

I spy

 a basket,

a 6 by a 3,

 a really strong man,

and a block with a G.

I spy two matching words.

 yellow umbrella

cave's yellow glow

craft stick

I spy two matching words.

 man with blue yarn

hat

 really strong man

I spy two words that start with the letter C.

lamb

 cane

cactus

I spy two words that start with the letters FL.

 flamingo

fireman

 flag

I spy two words that end with the letter T.

butterfly

 hat

basket

I spy two words that end
with the letters ER.

baseball player

painted flower

unicorn's horn

I spy two words that rhyme.

butterfly

 dog that's small

blue bow tie

I spy two rhymes.

 6 by a 3

block with a G

 red bull's-eye